Cuckoo Feathers

✿Simply Sarah✿

Cuckoo Feathers

by **Phyllis Reynolds Naylor**

illustrated by **Marcy Ramsey**

Marshall Cavendish

Marshall Cavendish Corporation
99 White Plains Road, Tarrytown, NY 10591
www.marshallcavendish.us

Library of Congress Cataloging-in-Publication Data
Naylor, Phyllis Reynolds.
Cuckoo feathers / by Phyllis Reynolds Naylor ; illustrated by Marcy Ramsey. — 1st ed.
p. cm. — (Simply Sarah)
Summary: When two pigeons that Sarah wants as pets move from her
Chicago apartment's window ledge to the building next door, Sarah tries
to figure out how to get them to come back.
ISBN-13: 978-0-7614-5285-0
ISBN-10: 0-7614-5285-0
[1. Pigeons—Fiction. 2. Apartment houses—Fiction. 3. Neighbors—Fiction.
4. Chicago (Ill.)—Fiction.] I. Ramsey, Marcy Dunn, ill. II. Title. III. Series:
Naylor, Phyllis Reynolds. Simply Sarah.
PZ7.N24Cuc 2006
[Fic]—dc22
2005021126

The text of this book is set in Souvenir.
The illustrations are rendered in ink and wash.

Printed in The United States of America
A Marshall Cavendish Chapter Book
First edition

2 4 6 5 3 1

Marshall Cavendish
Children

For Melissa
—*P.R.N.*

To my Dad, my favorite
cuckoo of all time
—*M.R.*

Contents

One

Making Faces

Sarah Simpson wanted to be anything but ordinary. Her father called her his "Idea Girl," and it was true. She did have good ideas sometimes. But right now she couldn't think of anything to have a good idea about!

Sometimes she just wished she could change skins. She was tired of white. At dinner she looked down at her plate. There was cauliflower for dinner. She did not like cauliflower. There were onions. She did not like onions. Her skin was the color of cauliflower and onions and mashed potatoes. Her friend Peter's skin was the color of chocolate pudding.

"I don't want to eat anything white," Sarah said.

"What?" asked Mom.

"I'm tired of white. I only want chocolate."

"Oh," said Mom. "Then I guess you don't ever want bread."

Sarah thought it over. She could live without bread.

"No more milk?" asked her little brother, Riley.

Sarah could live without milk.

"No more angel food cake?" asked Mom. "Are you sure you can give up that?"

Sarah swallowed.

"No more ice cream?" asked Riley.

"Just fooling," Sarah said with a sigh, and ate a bite of cauliflower. "But I wish *I* was a different color."

Mom laughed.

"What's so funny?" Sarah asked.

"You'll see," said Mom.

Sarah's mother was an artist, and the family lived in a fourth floor apartment in Chicago.

Sarah's father was overseas building bridges. The fourth floor was a loft, with a skylight in the ceiling. There were bookcases and screens in place of walls between rooms.

When dinner was over, Mom led Sarah and Riley back to her workplace at one end of the apartment.

Long tables held pages of the books her mother was illustrating. There were pictures propped against the wall, the paint still wet. There were splotches and splatters of red and purple and green all over the floor.

"Sit down," said Mom. Sarah sat on one side of a worktable and Riley sat on the other. Sarah's mother put little pots of paint in the center of the table—red and yellow and brown and white and black. She put a saucer in front of Riley and gave another to Sarah. She gave each of them a brush.

"Now," she said, "put a little bit of paint from the pots on your saucers. See if you can mix them up until you match the color of your own hand."

"Easy," said Sarah.

She dipped her brush in the white paint and put it on her saucer. Then she laid her hand next to it. They weren't the same color at all. Riley chose yellow. His hand didn't match yellow either.

"Keep trying," Mom said. "Add a little bit of this and a little of that until you come close to the color of your own skin."

Sarah added yellow to her white. It still wasn't right. She added a little red. Not right either. She mixed in a little brown, then white again. Then another dab of yellow. *Mix, mix, mix. Match, match, match.* It took four different colors to match the shade of her own skin.

Someone was knocking at the door. Riley ran to answer. When he came back, he had Peter with him. Peter lived in an apartment below with his grandmother.

"What are you doing? Painting pictures?" Peter asked.

"Painting hands," said Sarah. She gave Peter her saucer and brush. "How many colors will it take to make chocolate pudding?" she asked.

Peter smiled. He put black on his saucer. Too dark. He mixed in brown. Still too dark. He added yellow. Nope. Not right yet. A little red. A little white. *Mix, mix, mix. Match, match, match.* "It took four colors to make me," said Sarah.

"Ha! It took five colors to make me," said Peter.

"*Coo,*" came a call from the window ledge. Peter turned around.

"That's our pigeon!" said Sarah, pointing to the black pigeon with white on its tail. "We call her Coo." They went over to the window with Riley.

A second pigeon appeared, a brown one. "Then that must be Cuckoo," Peter said, and they laughed.

"*Coo, coo, uckle, uckle, uckle,*" went Coo, rubbing her bill against Cuckoo.

"Do they belong to you?" asked Peter.

"They just showed up one day, and they've been hanging around," Sarah told him. For a few minutes, she and Riley and Peter watched the pigeons walk back and forth on the window ledge with the low iron railing around it.

"Oh, look!" said Sarah.

A young boy in the next building was watching the pigeons too. Sarah waved.

The boy ran away from the window. When he came back, a girl was with him. She was older, about as old as Sarah. The boy pointed to Sarah and Riley and Peter. The girl waved back at Sarah, but the boy stuck out his tongue. Riley stuck out his tongue too.

"Don't," said Sarah.

But then Riley made a face. It was a terrible face. He pulled out his cheeks and pushed up his nose and rolled his eyes.

The girl across the alley made a face back. It was an even worse face than Riley's.

"I need a leg," called Mom from her drawing board. "I'm drawing a picture of a boy throwing a baseball. Peter, would you pose for me?"

Sarah and Peter left the window, and Mom gave Peter a ball of string.

"Pretend it's a baseball. Pretend you're the pitcher and you're winding up to throw a fastball," she said.

Peter pulled back his arm. He threw the ball of string against the wall.

"Would you do it again?" asked Mom. "I want to see what you do with your feet."

Riley got the ball of string, and Peter threw it again.

"One more time?" asked Mom.

Peter threw it once more.

"Thank you," Mom said. "You're a real help."

When Peter went back downstairs, Sarah returned to the window. Coo and Cuckoo were still there, but the boy and his sister were gone.

Two

The Kids Next Door

When Sarah got home from school the next day with Peter, they found Riley waiting for them inside the front entrance to their apartment building.

"What's up, Riley?" Peter said.

"Coo wants to come in," Riley told them. "She's been pecking at our window all day."

Just then a school bus stopped outside the building next door. It wasn't a bus from Sarah's school, and a little boy got off. The boy who made faces.

Sarah watched as the older girl got off next. She had long, shiny black hair and tiny gold earrings. *She must be the boy's big sister*, Sarah thought. She remembered the terrible face the girl had made back at Riley. The boy and girl opened the glass doors of their apartment building and went inside.

Suddenly Sarah started to smile. "Come on!" she said, pulling Riley outside. She and Riley and Peter ran over to the building next to theirs. They tapped on the glass. When the boy and girl turned around, Sarah made a crazy face. So did Peter and Riley. The boy and the girl with gold earrings made crazy faces too.

Sarah laughed. Then she and Peter and Riley went back to their own building.

"I wonder who they are," said Peter. "I'll bet they've just moved in."

On the third floor, Peter went into the apartment where he lived with his grandmother. Sarah and Riley climbed up to the fourth floor. When they walked into the loft and over to the window, the boy and the girl with the tiny gold earrings were looking at them from the building next door. They

were laughing too and making more faces. Sarah made her eyes go crossed and pulled at her ears.

Mom looked up from her drawing board, a pencil in her hand. "Do you know those children?" she asked.

"No," said Sarah.

"Then why are you making faces at them?"

"Because it's fun," Sarah told her.

"Well, stop," said Mom. "Besides, I need a hand."

Sarah went to help. When her mother said she needed a hand or a leg or a foot, she needed to see one in a certain position to know exactly how to draw it.

Sarah waited while Mom arranged her arm just so. Then she stood very still while her mother drew her arm and hand for the book she was illustrating.

Outside the window, Coo, the pigeon, strutted along the wide ledge with the low iron railing. Her dark eye watched as Mom drew Sarah's hand.

"Did you feed Coo this morning?" asked Sarah.

"Don't move," said Mom, busy with her pencil.

"I'm not," said Sarah. "But has Coo had anything to eat?"

"I put out a few crusts of bread, but pigeons need to look for food themselves. We don't want them to depend too much on people," Mom said.

Sarah sat very still. She wondered if the girl with the gold earrings had even noticed the pigeons that had been hanging around outside. Even more, however, Sarah wished that *she* had long, shiny black hair instead of ordinary brown. Then people would say, "Here comes Sarah Simpson, the girl with the beautiful hair!" She liked to be someone *special*.

"You know what I want for my birthday, Mom?" she asked, careful not to move an inch.

"What's that?"

"I want to get my ears pierced. I want

tiny gold earrings to wear to school."

"Don't even think it," said Mom.

"Why *not*?"

"Because you're too young. I didn't get my ears pierced till I was fifteen."

"Well, I'm not you!" said Sarah. "The girl next door has gold earrings!"

"And you're not the girl next door," said Mom.

Sarah sighed. At least Coo had been pecking at *their* window all day, not the window in the next building. Sarah could say that Coo was *her* pigeon, no matter what anyone thought. And that, come to think of it, was pretty special. It wasn't ordinary in the least. The next time anyone asked if she had a pet, she would say, "Sure! I've got a pigeon!"

It was Sarah's job to entertain four-year-old Riley for an hour each day while Mom was making dinner. Her mother paid her fifty cents an hour, and at the end of the week, Sarah got three dollars and fifty cents. Most of the time she spent it on books or ice cream.

That evening, when Mom was making spaghetti sauce and Sarah was caring for Riley, she quietly opened the window and let Coo come in.

"*Coo, coo, uckle, uckle, uckle,*" went the pigeon, fluttering down to the floor and walking about. It peeped under the sofa. It studied a chair. It pecked at a piece of fuzz on the floor. "*Coo, coo, uckle, uckle, uckle,*" it went.

Mom heard.

"Get that bird out of here," she called from the stove.

"Okay. Just a minute," said Sarah. She got a cracker and broke it into big crumbs. She dropped the pieces along the floor and up onto the windowsill.

Coo began to eat the crumbs.

"Is that bird gone?" called Mom.

Sarah and Riley hurried the pigeon toward the window.

"I'm counting," Mom said. "One . . . two . . . three . . ."

Coo hopped up on the windowsill, still pecking at the crumbs.

"Four . . . five . . . six . . . ." Mom continued.

Plop! The pigeon pooped.

Sarah quickly cleaned it up.

Three
Where's Home?

At school the next day, Sarah told Tim Wong and Emily Watson that she had a pet pigeon. *Two*, in fact!

"Where do you keep them?" Tim wanted to know.

"Right outside on the window ledge," said Sarah.

"What kind are they?" asked Emily.

Sarah had not thought about what kind. A pigeon was a pigeon, right? She tried to think of the different kinds of pigeons. "A homing pigeon," she said.

"What?" said Peter. "How do you know

those are homing pigeons? Homing pigeons carry messages strapped to their legs."

That was news to Sarah. "So we'll tape some messages to their legs," she said. Homing pigeons they were. Sarah, the Idea Girl! "Their names are Coo and Cuckoo."

In class, when Sarah was supposed to be looking up a question about presidents in the encyclopedia, she looked up "pigeon" instead. She read that they are very strong fliers. She read that they walk with their toes pointed inward. People who walk that way are said to be "pigeon-toed."

Most birds, the book said, tip their heads back after each sip when drinking. Pigeons, however, put their beaks in the water and pump the liquid down their throats. The pouter pigeon struts about with its neck puffed out like a balloon. The fantail pigeon dances on its toes.

"Sarah," said the teacher. "Did you find the answer?"

Sarah blinked. *What was the question?* she wondered.

"How was he different from the others?" the teacher asked.

"He . . . dances on his toes?" Sarah said, unable to remember what the class had been talking about in the first place.

Everyone stared. Then everyone laughed.

"President *Roosevelt?*" said the teacher.

Sarah's face turned fire-engine red.

"Peter, perhaps you can tell us," said Mrs. Gold.

"He proved that you can be a good president even when you're in a wheelchair," said Peter.

"Right," said the teacher. "Sarah, whatever you're reading, save it till recess, okay?"

All afternoon Sarah thought about turning Coo and Cuckoo into homing pigeons. The encyclopedia said that homing pigeons had carried messages during wartime. They would be taken to places hundreds of miles away.

Then they would fly back with messages strapped to their legs. Coo and Cuckoo came back every day, didn't they? Why couldn't Sarah train them to take messages back and forth to Tim Wong and Emily Watson?

Sarah was so excited by her new idea that she could hardly wait to get home that afternoon. But when she got back to her apartment, Coo and Cuckoo were not on the window ledge. Not on *her* window ledge. They were on the window ledge with the iron railing of the building next door.

It was the window where the boy who made faces lived, and the girl with the gold earrings. There was an old flowerpot on the ledge, a pot that had been left by the people who had lived there before. Coo and Cuckoo were flying back and forth with bits of straw and dry leaves and grass in their beaks.

"Do you see those pigeons?" asked Mom. "I've been watching them all day. I think they're making a nest in that old flowerpot."

NO! Sarah thought. *Not there, Coo! You're MY pigeons. You're supposed to be over here!*

"Let's put out a flowerpot so they'll make their nest here!" Sarah said.

"Why? They seem perfectly happy with that one," said her mother.

"But our window ledge is better!" Sarah said desperately. "We feed them!" How could she say that she didn't *want* the girl with the gold earrings to have her pigeons? How could she say that she didn't want the little brother making faces at Coo and Cuckoo through the window?

"I thought . . . I thought they liked it here! If you had let them come in and walk around every day, they would have built their nest on *our* window ledge!" said Sarah angrily.

Mom looked up from her drawing. "I don't think so, Sarah. You can still put out food for them, you know. There's no reason the pigeons can't come over here for a meal now and then."

It wasn't the same. Where pigeons went to eat was more like a restaurant. Where they went to sleep was more like home.

Sarah went to the refrigerator and took out an old piece of bread. She found some leftover peas and a strip of bacon. She started at one end of their apartment, opening a window and putting some of the food on the window ledge. Then she went to the next window and the next and the next.

"What are you doing?" asked Riley, coming out of the bedroom with his dump truck.

"Showing the pigeons where they belong," Sarah said.

"Where do they belong?" asked Riley.

"Here. They're *our* pigeons! They were pecking at our window. You said so!"

Riley looked at Coo and Cuckoo building a nest in the flowerpot next door.

"Maybe they like it better over there," he said.

And that was when Sarah decided to use her money to buy the pigeons an even bigger, better flowerpot, a brand-new one just for them.

Four
Flowerpot Blues

First of all, Sarah needed to know how much a flowerpot would cost. A *big* flowerpot.

Peter's grandmother went to the store on Saturdays, and Sarah would ask her. Granny Belle made Peter go with her and pull his wagon so that they could bring home all the food they had bought. Peter hated the wagon. He hated going to the store because the wagon made a lot of noise and people turned to look.

On Saturday, Sarah got up early. She opened her apartment door and went out in the hall so she could look down at Peter's

apartment. The newspaper outside his door had not been taken in. That meant Granny Belle was still sleeping.

Sarah put on her navy blue pants and her green and white T-shirt. She ate her cereal by the open door of her apartment. Halfway through her cereal, she heard a door open. She set her bowl on the floor and darted out in the hall to look. She was just in time to see Peter's Batman pajamas go back inside with the newspaper.

But fifteen minutes later, she heard the door open again. She ran out into the hall. Peter and Granny Belle were going down to the second floor, carrying the wagon. Peter was holding the back end, and his grandmother was holding the handle.

"Wait!" Sarah called.

Granny Belle stopped and turned around. She was wearing her sturdy black shoes. She had a blue hat on her head with a blue and white bow. Her black and gray pocketbook was tucked under one arm.

"Good morning, Sarah!" she said.

"You want to pull this wagon?" Peter asked.

"Not really," Sarah said. "I just want to ask a favor. Could you look at flowerpots while you're at the store and see how much they cost?"

"Flowerpots?" said Granny Belle. "Who's planting flowers with fall on the way?"

"It's sort of a surprise," said Sarah. "I need a great big flowerpot."

"I don't know if the store sells flowerpots, but I'll ask," said Granny Belle. She and Peter went on clanking and clunking down the stairs until they got to the ground floor. Out the door they went.

Sarah went back upstairs, pleased with her idea. What bird *wouldn't* want a brand-new flowerpot for a nest? It was certainly nicer than an old, cracked, leftover pot that had been sitting out in the wind and rain for a long time.

When Riley woke up, Sarah made a piece of toast for him and spread it with peanut butter. She poured his milk. But later, when she heard Peter's wagon come clanking and clunking back into the lobby downstairs, she ran to the door of her apartment. She watched for him over the railing. First, Peter and his grandmother carried their grocery sacks up. Then, they carried the wagon up.

"Did you see any big flowerpots?" Sarah called down. "Did you find out how much they cost?"

"Seven dollars and ninety-eight cents," Granny Belle called back up.

"Thank you!" Sarah said.

She checked the box in her drawer where she kept her money. Only fifty-one cents. It would take more than two weeks to earn enough money to buy the flowerpot. That wasn't soon enough.

Mom came out to the kitchen in her robe and made herself some coffee. She had a smudge of yellow paint in her hair.

"If I took care of Riley for an extra hour each day for a week, could you pay me twice as much?" Sarah asked her.

"For a whole week? I think maybe I could do that," said Mom.

"I don't need anyone to take care of me!" Riley insisted. "I can take care of myself."

"Of course," said Sarah, "but we could do fun things together, okay?"

"Okay," said Riley. Sarah and her mother exchanged smiles.

Maybe she could buy the big flowerpot before Coo and Cuckoo finished building their nest, Sarah thought. Maybe they would see the new pot and start building their nest over here. Maybe she could even put some dry grass and leaves in it and get a nest started for them. While Riley was getting dressed, Sarah walked over to the window that looked out at the building next door.

Her heart sank. The nest in the old flowerpot seemed to be done. Coo, the black pigeon with white on her tail, was sitting on it. Right there on the neighbors' window ledge, she looked perfectly at home.

Grass and twigs and leaves stuck up all around her—a rather messy-looking nest—but Coo didn't seem to mind. And perched on the little iron railing next to her was Cuckoo, holding a bug in his beak.

Sarah felt tears welling up in her eyes. Her nose began to sting. It wasn't fair! She had fed those pigeons. She had even let Coo come inside! Why couldn't they have built their nest over here?

Just then the girl with the gold earrings appeared in the window. She didn't see Sarah watching her. The girl was watching the pigeons. Sarah saw her turn around and talk to someone, and then a man came to the window. He and the girl watched the pigeons together.

All at once the girl saw Sarah. For a few seconds they just stared at each other. Then the girl smiled and pointed to the nest with Coo in it. But Sarah turned away and went to the bathroom to blow her nose.

She wouldn't have homing pigeons after all. She wouldn't even have pigeons. Her window ledge wasn't special. *She* wasn't special. Sarah was just an ordinary, everyday girl looking out an ordinary, everyday window at pigeons who didn't even have enough sense to know where they were really wanted.

Sarah had the Flowerpot Blues, and it really hurt.

Five

Phone Call From Dad

It was an awful Saturday. An awful weekend! Riley didn't want to do anything Sarah suggested. He didn't want to listen to any of his tapes. Didn't want to read his dinosaur book. Didn't want to build a castle or work a puzzle.

"All *you* do is look out the window!" he complained to Sarah. That was true.

Sarah had put popcorn kernels on all the window ledges outside their apartment. If only Coo and Cuckoo would leave their nest. If only they would come back here, she would give them anything they wanted.

She'd even collect bugs for them if she had to.

She tried to stay cheerful for her father's phone call on Sunday. Every Sunday evening her father called from across the ocean and talked to each of them.

When it was Sarah's turn, she said, "Guess what, Dad? I have two pigeons, Coo and Cuckoo!"

"Really?" said her dad. "Pet pigeons?"

"Not exactly, but I'm going to train them to be homing pigeons and carry messages," Sarah said bravely. Her mother raised her eyebrows. "That's my new big idea."

This time her father laughed. "How are you going to do that, Idea Girl?" he asked.

"I don't know, but you can fasten a message on a homing pigeon's leg and take it far away. It will always fly home again," Sarah told him. "Wouldn't it be great if I could train them to carry a message to you?"

"Now that really would be something," her father said. "But in the meantime, I guess the telephone will have to do."

Sarah gave the telephone back to her mother. She knew the pigeons could never carry messages to her father. She probably wouldn't be able to get them to carry messages to her friends. In fact, she might not even be able to get them to leave their nest next door and come to her *own* window ledge.

Sarah went into the bathroom, took off her clothes, and climbed into the tub. She ran the water so high and sank down so low that only her eyes and nose were sticking out. Water throbbed in her ears. Nobody but Sarah thought of the pigeons as pets. What was the use of being the Idea Girl if nobody believed in your idea?

She thought about the girl with the gold earrings. She remembered the way she had pointed at Coo in the nest. If Coo laid eggs and they hatched, the baby pigeons would grow up right outside the girl's window, not hers. Sarah couldn't stand it.

She shut her eyes and tipped back her head. She sank even lower in the water, so that only her nose was sticking out. At last she let out her breath through her mouth. A long string of bubbles ruffled the surface of the water.

Slowly Sarah rose up, her hair streaming wet, drops clinging to her eyelashes.

Tomorrow . . . maybe . . . she would ask the girl's name.

But when tomorrow came, Sarah didn't feel any better. She didn't smile as she put on her clothes. She didn't smile as she ate her cereal. She didn't even look out the window. It only made her sad to see her pigeons on a nest next door.

Sarah slipped her backpack onto her shoulders and went downstairs to wait for Peter. As they walked to school he told her about his weekend.

"First, we took a bus over to my aunt's house," he said. "Then, we all walked to the lake. We took a boat ride out on Lake Michigan. Then, we went to a museum."

"And I suppose you had ice cream afterward," Sarah said, sulking.

"Pizza *and* ice cream!" said Peter. "What did *you* do?"

"Took a bath," said Sarah in a dull, flat voice. "Let's don't talk about it."

At school, she wished she had never told anyone about the pigeons.

"How are Coo and Cuckoo?" asked Tim Wong.

"They're okay," Sarah said.

"Have they had any babies yet?" asked Emily.

"Not yet," Sarah mumbled. She stuck her face in her history book.

By the time school was out, Sarah had made up her mind. When she and Peter reached their building, he went on up to his apartment. Sarah stayed outside. She waited on the sidewalk and finally saw it coming— the yellow school bus with *St. Mary's School* on the side in black letters.

Six

Hot Cocoa

Sarah watched as the bus stopped outside the building next door. She waited while the boy who made faces and the girl with the gold earrings got off. Then Sarah took a deep breath and walked over.

"Hi," she said.

The boy and girl turned around. The boy made a face, but the girl didn't.

"Hi," said the girl.

"I'm Sarah," Sarah told them, and pointed to her building. "I live on the top floor with my mom and my brother, Riley."

"I'm Mercedes," said the girl with the shiny black hair. "And this is my cousin Leon. I live with him and my aunt and uncle."

"Want to come over?" Sarah invited.

"I'll ask," said Mercedes. "But I'll have to bring Leon."

Leon made another face.

"Sure," said Sarah.

She waited while Mercedes and Leon went into their building. It seemed strange that Mercedes should be named after a car, but Sarah didn't care. Mercedes could have been named after a truck or a bus or a boat or a plane and Sarah wouldn't have minded. She only cared that Mercedes would be willing to share the pigeons.

"We can come!" Mercedes said when they ran back out again. "But your mother has to call my aunt when we get up to your place."

"Okay," Sarah said. She smiled as she led the way to the loft.

On the third floor, they stopped at Peter's apartment. Sarah knocked on the door. "This is where Peter Grant lives," she said. "He's my friend too."

Granny Belle answered the door. She had a green sweater around her shoulders and slippers with tassels on her feet.

"Hello, Sarah," she said. "What do we have here?"

"Two new neighbors," Sarah told her. "Mercedes and Leon. We're going upstairs. Can Peter come too?"

Peter pushed past his grandmother to see who was at the door. He was eating a doughnut and had frosting on his nose.

"After he washes his face and hands, he can," said Granny Belle. She smiled at Mercedes and Leon. "Welcome to the neighborhood," she said.

Upstairs, Sarah opened the door to the loft. Riley ran to meet her. He stared at the visitors. Mercedes and Leon, in turn, stared at the strange apartment with a skylight in the ceiling and bookcases and screens in place of walls.

"This is where my mom works. She's an artist," said Sarah. "My dad works overseas."

"It sure is big," said Mercedes, looking around.

"It sure smells funny," said Leon, making a face.

"It smells like paint," said Riley. He made a face back.

Mom came out from behind the bookcases at the end of the loft. "Hello," she said.

Sarah introduced her new friends.

"They live over there," Sarah said, pointing to the window in the next building. "Mercedes wants you to call her aunt."

Mom looked out the window. Mercedes' aunt was looking out the window of the building next door.

Sarah's mother opened the window. "I'm Amber, Sarah's mother," she called. "We're glad to have Mercedes and Leon visit us."

"I'm Gloria Mendez," the aunt called back. "They can stay for an hour, but if they're any trouble, please send them home."

"I'm sure they'll be fine," said Mom. She turned around. "Would anyone like some hot chocolate?"

Everyone said yes. When Peter came up, he said yes too.

"What do you like with your cocoa?" Mom asked. "Marshmallows?"

"I like mine with cinnamon," Mercedes said.

"I like mine with chocolate sprinkles," said Leon.

"We like ours with whipped cream," Sarah told them.

Everyone wanted to try cocoa with marshmallows and cinnamon and whipped cream and sprinkles. As Mom set the cups on the table she said, "Mercedes is a beautiful name. And those are pretty earrings. Where did you get them?"

"In Mexico," said Mercedes.

"Have you been to Mexico?" asked Sarah.

"That's where I was born," Mercedes told her.

"Have you been watching the pigeons?" asked Mom. "They've built a nest in the old flowerpot outside your window. We can see them from here. I'm sure there are eggs in it by now."

"Yes. My aunt says that pigeons are good luck," Mercedes said.

When Mom went back to her painting, Riley took Leon into his bedroom to show him all his trucks. Sarah and Peter and Mercedes stayed at the table and talked about mice in the apartments and school and snow.

"If you want a good restaurant, try Wongs'," Sarah told her new friend. "They have the very best chicken wings in all of Chicago."

"Come over sometime and you can see the pigeons up close," Mercedes said when it was time to go. "I'll ask my aunt to make some tostados."

Sarah didn't know what tostados were, but she was sure they would be delicious. Anything with a name like that would have to be wonderful.

That evening at dinner, Sarah frowned at her meat loaf.

"Why didn't you name me something unusual, like Buick or Plymouth? Plymouth would be a pretty name for a girl," she said.

"I named you Sarah because I like it," said Mom. "And Mercedes' name has nothing to do with cars."

Sarah knew her voice sounded grumpy, and she knew that her grumpiness had nothing to do with cars either. It had to do with pigeons. It had everything to do with pigeons. She just couldn't get over the fact that Coo and Cuckoo lived on the neighbors' window ledge, and that the girl who loved them most—Sarah Simpson—had lost out.

Seven

Scrambled Babies

It was Sarah who saw the eggs first. She had been eating her toast by the window and watching the pigeons. Mom was packing her lunch for school.

Coo was sitting on the nest as usual. Cuckoo was strutting back and forth on top of the little iron railing as usual. Sarah and Riley were eating breakfast as usual. It was an ordinary morning in the city.

Then Coo got off the nest and Sarah saw them: two white eggs.

"Look!" Sarah shouted. "I can see the eggs now, Mom! There are two eggs in Coo's nest!"

Her mother hurried over to see, and so did Riley.

"They're going to have babies!" Sarah told Riley, "and Coo and Cuckoo are the parents."

Cuckoo flew in and took his turn on the nest. He didn't seem too gentle.

"He'll break them!" said Riley.

"No, I'm sure he'll be careful," Mom said.

Sarah hoped that Mercedes would look out the window before going to school. And sure enough, the light came on in the kitchen next door. The girl with the gold earrings appeared at the window. She saw Sarah, and both girls opened their window.

"There are eggs in the nest!" Sarah called. "Two eggs! I saw them!"

"Hooray!" shouted Mercedes. "We're going to be grandparents!" The girls laughed.

When Sarah sat down again, Mom said, "You'd better finish your breakfast, Sarah. Peter will be waiting for you."

Riley sat back down too. "How do you

know there are going to be babies?" he asked Sarah.

"Because birds lay eggs and baby birds hatch out of eggs," Sarah told him. She had to explain everything to Riley.

Riley looked down at the scrambled eggs on his plate.

"Scrambled babies," he said.

"Those are not babies, they're eggs," said Mom.

"They might be babies if I didn't eat them," said Riley.

"They're *eggs*! Don't be silly," Mom said.

"Maybe they'll turn into babies in my stomach," said Riley.

Mom sighed. "Are you going to eat breakfast or not?"

"Not eggs," said Riley.

Sarah could hardly wait to get to school. She threw on her jacket and stuffed her lunch in her backpack. She ran down the stairs to the third floor. Granny Belle opened the door when she knocked.

"Peter's brushing his teeth," said Granny Belle. "Come in."

"I have a secret!" Sarah said excitedly. "But I want to tell Peter myself."

Granny Belle bent down low. "Any secrets go in this ear, they never come out again," she said.

So Sarah told her about the two eggs.

"Just what we need in this city. More pigeons," the old woman said.

Peter came out of his bedroom carrying his Batman lunch box.

"Have a good day at school," Granny Belle told them.

Out on the sidewalk, Sarah said, "I know a secret. Want to guess?"

"Loose tooth?" asked Peter.

"No."

"Brownies for lunch?"

"Nope."

"A hole in your underwear?" asked Peter.

Sarah shoved him and laughed. "No. It's eggs."

"In your lunch sack?"

"In Coo's nest! Coo and Cuckoo are taking turns sitting on them!"

"Wow!" said Peter. "Are you going to eat them when they hatch?"

Sarah stopped walking and stared at Peter. "No!" she said, almost shouting. "Are you crazy?"

Peter shrugged. "Baby pigeons are called squabs. Some people say they're really good!"

"Well, *we're* not going to eat them!" Sarah cried, but all the way to school, she worried. They weren't outside *her* window. They were over at the Mendezes' place. If Mercedes Mendez ate something called tostados, maybe her family ate squabs as well.

When school was out that day, Sarah stopped with Peter at his apartment. Granny Belle said to Sarah, "*I* have a secret too! Only it's more of a surprise."

"What is it?" asked Sarah.

Granny Belle went into the kitchen and came back with a large clay flowerpot. "These were on sale at half price, so I bought it for you. You can pay me whenever you like."

Oh, no! Sarah stared at the pot. She didn't need it now! Coo and Cuckoo would never use it, not with two eggs waiting to hatch in the other flowerpot. She knew that Granny Belle was trying to be kind. She thanked her and went upstairs to get her money. She hid the flowerpot under her bed before her mother and Riley could see it.

The flowerpot made her sad, however. It would have been so much fun to have had the pigeons over here. It would have been so much fun to have watched the babies hatch out of the eggs and learn to fly. To see it all from her own window. How could she even call them hers anymore? They belonged to the Mendez family, if, of course, they belonged to anyone at all.

Eight

Trouble

Everyone began coming up to Sarah's apartment each day after school to watch the pigeons and wait for the eggs to hatch.

"What's this? The Cocoa Club?" Mom asked, laughing, when she found them sitting at the table once again.

"Leon's baby brother is sleeping, so we all came here to watch the pigeons," Sarah explained. "And Mercedes says they would never ever eat them."

"Well, I should hope not!" said Mom.

"Uncle Carlos said that baby pigeons are really, really ugly," said Mercedes.

"But we still wouldn't eat them," added Leon.

"That's good," said Mom.

She had just poured the cocoa into cups and placed the marshmallows on the table when there was a terrible screeching noise outside.

Everyone crowded near the window. A large gray pigeon that Sarah had not seen before flew around the corner of the building. Cuckoo was just behind him, hitting at him with his wings as if to knock him right out of the sky.

With a flutter of wings, dipping and diving, the two birds flew through the narrow space between the two buildings. Then they made a U-turn and flew back out again.

"That bad bird is fighting Cuckoo!" cried Riley.

The birds turned again. This time when they came back, the new bird dive-bombed the nest. Sarah screamed. The gray pigeon gave Coo a peck on the head before Cuckoo drove him off again.

Sarah threw open the window.

"Bad bird!" she shouted, waving her arms.

"Get out of here!" yelled Peter.

"Go away!" shouted Mercedes, tossing her cocoa at him.

Riley threw a handful of marshmallows.

Coo turned her head nervously on the nest. She looked first one way, then the other.

Mom stuck her head out the window just in time to see the new bird take another dive at Coo. "He's trying to drive Coo out of the nest, I think," she said. "He probably wants that nest for himself."

"Well, he can't have it!" cried Sarah. "Coo and Cuckoo got there first."

When the strange bird came back again, Mom grabbed a towel and flapped it out the window. This time the new bird flew away.

"I'm afraid he'll come back, though," Mom said.

"Then we'll have to take turns guarding

the nest," said Sarah. "Don't worry, Coo. We'll protect you from Bad Bird."

But Bad Bird didn't come back that afternoon.

Cuckoo seemed to know that the danger was over. He walked back and forth on the low iron railing. He made strange noises in his throat. Then he hopped down to smooth Coo's feathers where she had been pecked.

"What if Bad Bird comes while we're asleep?" asked Riley.

"What if he comes while I'm at school?" asked Sarah.

"I don't know," said Mom. "We can't watch out the window all the time."

Mercedes' aunt appeared in the window next door.

Mom called over to her. "Gloria, did you see what happened?"

"That other bird has been hanging around all day," Mrs. Mendez called back.

"We chased him away," called Sarah. "Mom waved a towel."

"I threw cocoa at him," Mercedes called.

"I threw marshmallows!" said Riley.

"But how can we keep him away for good?" Peter asked.

Nobody knew.

When everyone had gone home, Sarah went down to the basement to talk to Mr. Gurdy. He was the man who took care of the building. He was short and square and had a stiff mustache that curled up at the ends.

"What's the problem?" he asked.

"A pigeon is the problem," Sarah told him.

"Pigeons are always a problem," said Mr. Gurdy.

Sarah told him about Coo and Cuckoo and the new gray pigeon that was causing trouble.

"So what do you want me to do about it?" asked Mr. Gurdy. "I'm not doing the pecking. And besides, that nest is next door."

Sarah knew she would get no help from Mr. Gurdy. But then he added, more kindly,

"Even if I was to put up something to scare that bird away, it might frighten your other pigeons too. Coo might never come back to her nest."

That was something Sarah hadn't thought of before. As she went back upstairs, she met Granny Belle coming down with a load of laundry. Sarah told her what had happened with the pigeons that afternoon.

Granny Belle nodded. "Sometimes," she said, "the best thing is to let pigeons take care of themselves. Sometimes they know what to do better than we do."

"But if he drives Coo out of the nest and the eggs don't hatch, then what?" asked Sarah.

"Then Coo and Cuckoo will have to start all over again," said Granny Belle.

Sarah found it hard to sleep that night. The Idea Girl should be able to think of *something*!

It happened the next day. Sarah and Peter walked home together. They waited until the bus from St. Mary's School pulled up. Mercedes and Leon got out. This time Mercedes was wearing tiny gold earrings in the shape of a cross. All four of them went upstairs to Sarah's. Mercedes and Leon went to the window to wave to Leon's mother. Mrs. Mendez liked to know that they were home safely.

At that very moment, however, Bad Bird swooped down between the two buildings once again. Both Coo and Cuckoo went after him, flapping their wings and pecking at him. They all squawked loudly.

As the three birds turned and came back again, Bad Bird dived toward the nest in the flowerpot. He nudged one of the eggs closer to the edge of the pot.

"He's trying to push it out of the nest!" screamed Sarah.

She and Peter opened the window partway. They all stuck their hands through the opening. They threw Fruit Loops and raisins at the gray pigeon. Mom flapped a dish towel.

But it did no good. The next time Bad Bird flew past the window, he dived once again toward the flowerpot. With his long beak, he gave the egg another push. This time it rolled over the rim of the pot. It dropped straight down over the edge of the window ledge and onto the cement far below.

Nine

Poem for a Bird

Sarah stared in horror. Peter and Mercedes gasped. Riley began to cry.

"Oh, no!" Mom said softly.

Sarah turned blindly from the window and ran from the loft. Down the stairs she went to third, with her friends following after her. Down the stairs to second she went. On down to first.

She burst through the doors at the front entrance and ran around to the narrow alley between the two buildings. There on the concrete was Coo's egg. The shell had been broken. The pieces were scattered.

And there among the pieces of shell was a tiny bird with no feathers at all. It was dead.

Everyone felt like crying. Sarah could hear Peter swallowing again and again.

"I wish I could kill Bad Bird!" Leon said angrily. "I would break his bones into a million pieces!"

"We should throw rocks at him!" said Peter.

"We should drown him," said Mercedes.

Silently, gently, Sarah scooped up the little dead bird. She carefully carried it upstairs, surrounded by her friends.

"This is so sad," said Mom. "I'm sure it would have been a beautiful bird."

Sarah could hardly stand it. It was about one of the saddest days of her life. Almost as sad as the day her father left for overseas.

On the ledge next door, Coo and Cuckoo seemed very nervous.

Coo was sitting on the egg that was left. She kept getting up and tucking it farther beneath her as though she was trying to protect it extra well.

Cuckoo paced back and forth on the railing, making loud noises. He looked first one way, then the other. He had scared off Bad Bird for now, but he didn't seem too sure of it. Who knew when Bad Bird would be back for the second egg?

"Why did he do it?" Sarah asked, her voice trembling.

"I think he's trying to drive Coo and Cuckoo away," said Mom. "Maybe he thinks that if their eggs are gone, they'll give up. They'll let him have the flowerpot for himself."

"Don't ever give up!" Peter called through the half-open window.

"Don't leave the egg alone, not even for a minute!" called Mercedes.

"That must be what happened," Mom told them. "The new bird was waiting for a chance to find the eggs alone."

Everyone looked sadly at the little dead bird on the table.

"I want to bury it," said Sarah. "I didn't want to just leave Coo's baby down in the alley. But it's got to be in a box or something."

Mom found a large matchbox. Sarah wrapped the little bird in a tissue. She slid it inside the box.

"Now we have to say a prayer," said Mercedes. "What kind of a prayer do you say for a bird?"

"Maybe it could be a poem," said Mom.

For a long time Sarah and her friends sat at the table, chins in their hands. They tried to think of a poem for a dead bird.

How could words help? Sarah wondered. They could never bring Coo's baby back again. They could never show all Sarah's anger toward Bad Bird. They could never show all her sadness.

"If you weren't dead, you'd move your head," said Peter at last.

Mercedes tried next: "Oh, little pigeon, soft and gray, I wish you'd lived another day."

"That's beautiful," said Mom.

"I would have fed you Cheerios, and watched you stand on your toes," said Leon.

"I would have given you a worm, and not let the sun burn," said Riley.

It was Sarah's turn: "I wish you'd lived to see your mother, and sit in the nest beside your brother."

"Which poem should we use?" asked Mercedes.

"I think they're all good. Let's put them together," said Mom.

She got a paper and wrote all the poems down, mixing them up a little. Then everyone read the poem aloud together. All except Riley, who couldn't read, and Leon, who didn't know some of the words:

To a Pigeon

I wish you'd lived to see your mother,
And sit in the nest beside your brother.
I would have given you a worm,
And not let the sun burn.

71

I would have fed you Cheerios,
And watched you stand on your toes.
If you weren't dead,
You'd move your head.
Oh, little pigeon, soft and gray,
I wish you'd lived another day.

They all trooped downstairs and out the back door of the building to the trees behind it. Sarah had brought a large spoon to dig a hole, and Peter put the matchbox down in it. They covered it up with dirt.

"Now we need a cross," said Mercedes. "I think I'll leave one of my earrings . . ."

Sarah couldn't believe it. Mercedes would leave an earring? But she removed it from her ear and stuck it down into the soft earth over the grave. Maybe she loved the pigeons almost as much as Sarah did.

"What do you suppose we would have named it if it had lived?" asked Sarah.

"Fog," said Peter.

"Fog?" asked Mercedes.

"Yes. Because it was soft and gray," Peter told them.

They all said good-bye to Fog and went sadly back inside.

Sarah went to bed angry that night, and she woke up angry again in the morning. Every time she thought of Bad Bird and what he had done, she wanted to do something awful right back to him.

Throwing water at him wouldn't be enough.

Throwing stones at him wouldn't be enough.

Sometimes she felt that she wanted to grab him and pull out all his feathers. Wring his neck and throw him in the river.

After school that day, the five children gathered in Peter's apartment to watch Granny Belle make cookies. They were large, flat cookies with sugar sprinkles on top. As they ate, Peter told his grandmother he would like to build a trap to catch Bad Bird.

"It could be the kind of trap where a door closes after the bird's inside," said Peter.

"Then we could drown him!" said Sarah.

"Chop him in pieces!" said Riley.

"Burn him!" said Mercedes.

"Hit him with rocks!" said Leon.

Granny Belle sat down at the table to rest her feet. She was drinking a cup of tea. "I don't think so," she said.

"You don't think what?" asked Peter.

"I don't think that doing something ugly to that pigeon is going to solve a thing," said his grandmother. "And you five children are sure talking ugly."

"But look what he did to Coo's egg!" said Sarah.

"I know," said Granny Belle, nodding her head. Her hair was as soft and gray as the little bird that had never lived. "But he only wanted a nest."

"It was *Coo's* nest!" cried Sarah and Peter together.

"How do you know it wasn't *his* nest before Coo and Cuckoo got there?" asked Granny Belle. "How do you know that Bad Bird might not have had that flower-pot first some time ago? That Coo and Cuckoo might not have come and chased *him* away?"

Sarah didn't know, because her family had only lived here for two years. Peter and his grandmother had been here for one year, and Mercedes had just moved in a month ago.

"Then they're *all* bad birds!" said Riley.

"No, I think they are just doing what birds do. And just like people, they want the best place for their babies," Granny Belle said.

Sarah lay awake a long time that night. She listened to the horns and whistles in the street below. She listened to fire engines and church bells and the striking of a clock. She listened to all the sounds of night in the city. Finally, just before she fell asleep, she knew what she was going to do.

Ten

Beaker and Sneaker

Early Saturday morning Sarah got up. She pulled the new clay pot out from under her bed. She went downstairs and out the front door.

Autumn was coming to Chicago. Sarah could feel it in the wind. The flag on the hotel down the street stuck straight out. In another month or two, snowflakes would be swirling in the air.

She went around the building to the trees out back. She picked up twigs and old grass and dry leaves and pressed them down inside the flowerpot. When she went back inside, she stopped in the laundry room. She took the lint that had collected in all the dryers. That would help make a soft nest for a pigeon.

Back in the apartment, Sarah pushed open the kitchen window. She placed the clay pot on the wide window ledge with the low iron railing around it. She put a handful of Cheerios on the ledge and closed the window. It seemed strange that now she *wanted* Bad Bird to come along. *Wanted* him to take over the new flowerpot.

Across the way, Coo sat on her egg, making sure that the last little bird would live. After a while, Cuckoo flew back to the nest and took his turn on the egg. But no Bad Bird came along. Riley woke up and came to the table for cereal. Sarah told him what she had done. For a long time they watched, but there was no sign of the gray pigeon.

"Oh, no!" Sarah said suddenly.

Coo had come over to Sarah's window ledge and was eating the Cheerios.

"Maybe she's going to lay another egg in *our* flowerpot!" said Riley.

"She can't have them both!" cried Sarah. "That's not fair!" But maybe what seemed fair to people was different for pigeons.

Coo finally flew back to her own nest. She took over the egg again while Cuckoo walked back and forth on the iron railing. Now and then he stopped to smooth his feathers. And then . . . around the corner came Bad Bird.

Mom walked into the kitchen just then to see what all the excitement was about. Sarah explained about giving the new flowerpot to Bad Bird.

"I think that's a fine idea, Sarah," her mother said.

First Bad Bird flew through the space between the buildings. Cuckoo was right behind him, trying to hit him with his wings. For a while it seemed that Cuckoo had driven away Bad Bird. But then the new pigeon flew right down and landed on the kitchen window ledge not three feet from where Sarah was sitting.

She didn't move. She didn't breathe.

"Sit as still as a statue, Riley," Mom whispered.

Bad Bird didn't seem to notice the flowerpot. He didn't even seem to notice the Cheerios. He was preening his feathers, as though a nest was the very last thing on his mind. Then he flew away without even a look at it.

"All that work for nothing," Sarah said.

"He didn't even see it," said Riley.

They were just about to leave the window when suddenly Bad Bird flew back. This time he wasn't alone.

Another gray pigeon, this one with white on her tail, landed on the window ledge beside him. They strutted to the left and then to the right. They were like soldiers in a parade, looking about and making a *coo, coo, uckle, uckle, uckle* sound in their throats.

Over at the other building, Coo nervously settled over her egg. Cuckoo flew back and forth between the buildings, swooping toward the new arrivals. But Bad Bird and his friend did not move from Sarah's ledge. Bad Bird found a bug and ate it.

And then, while Sarah and her mother and Riley watched, Bad Bird's friend hopped up on the edge of the new flowerpot and looked inside.

Sarah smiled at Mom. Mom smiled at Riley. Riley smiled out the window at Mercedes and Leon. They had come to their window across the way.

Bad Bird hopped up on the edge of the flowerpot too and looked inside. He picked up a piece of the soft lint from the dryer as though to inspect it. He dropped it down again and tucked it more securely among the twigs inside the pot.

Across the way, Cuckoo was making warning sounds. Again he flew swiftly between the two buildings. Bad Bird and his friend both flew away.

Will it work? Sarah wondered. *Will they come back?*

All day long Sarah watched for the pigeons.

She played with Riley and made sandwiches for lunch. Mom was hard at work on her newest pictures. She didn't mind when Peter came up later to show Sarah his book of puzzles and mazes.

But Sarah wasn't interested in puzzles on paper. She was interested in the puzzle of pigeons. There was only one more hour of daylight left. Soon it would be dark. Lights would come on in all the windows. The flag would be lowered at the hotel up the street. It would be too dark to look for pigeons then.

At that very moment, Bad Bird returned. He had a twig in his beak, and he dropped it in the new flowerpot. Sarah and Peter and Riley stood motionless just inside. Their eyes didn't even blink.

The other gray pigeon came back too. She also had a twig in her beak, or perhaps it was string. Into the flowerpot it went.

Across the way, Mrs. Mendez was holding her baby, Leon's little brother, and smiling. Mercedes and Leon were watching too.

Somehow the large gray pigeon didn't seem quite so bad anymore. He seemed more like a father bird wanting a good home for his children.

"I think we should give him a new name," said Sarah.

"What about Beaker, because of his big beak?" said Peter.

"Beaker and Sneaker, because she sort of sneaked in here before we even knew she was around," said Sarah.

So Beaker and Sneaker it was.

When Sarah's father called on Sunday evening, Sarah was still a little sad. She told him about Bad Bird and how he had pushed Coo's egg out of the nest.

"That's really a shame," her father said. "Sometimes I see sad things too."

"But guess what, Dad!" she said more happily. "Bad Bird has a home!" Then she explained how she had given the new flowerpot to Beaker and Sneaker, and changed their names as well.

"Extraordinary!" said her father. "Sarah, you are full of good ideas!"

Ten days later, Sarah looked out the window as usual. Beaker and Sneaker were taking turns sitting on their nest in the new flower-pot, as usual. But Coo and Cuckoo were nowhere to be seen.

In their place, in the old flowerpot next door, sat a tiny bird all alone. Its little neck was stretched high, its yellow beak wide open.

"Ohhhh!" cried Sarah, staring in wonder at the downy little bird bobbing about in the nest. A moment later, Coo appeared with a bug in her beak. And after she had fed her baby, Cuckoo came by with a worm.

"Mom!" Sarah called. "Riley! Come and see!"

Mom and Riley hurried to the window.

"Oh, just look!" said Mom. "There it is! Their baby!"

Sarah rushed to the telephone and called Mercedes. She giggled and said:

"Go to the window
And close your eyes.
Then open them up
And see a surprise!"

She heard Mercedes put down the phone. She heard her footsteps running on the floor. A moment later, Mercedes appeared at the window next door, and her eyes opened as wide as two coat buttons. Then she came back to the telephone.

"A baby!" she cried. "If its feathers turn out to be brown, guess what I'm going to call it? Cocoa!"

Sarah laughed.

And then one Saturday morning, very early, Sarah was once again eating her usual cereal in her usual place by the window. When she looked out, it was Beaker and Sneaker who were nowhere to be seen.

In their place, in the *new* flowerpot right outside her very window, sat two tiny birds all alone. Their little necks were stretched high, their yellow beaks open wide. The baby birds had hatched, and Sarah and Mercedes had become "grandparents" after all.

Sarah did not move. She did not even breathe. Mom and Riley were still asleep, so she didn't try to call to them. In that special moment, the sun was just beginning to peep over the roof of the building next door, and Sarah whispered softly, "Maybe I'll call you Sun and Shine."

Sarah smiled. She had given a flowerpot to a pigeon she hadn't wanted to like. Because of that, two pigeon families were friends. Two people families were friends.

And who knew what would happen next?